MISTER BILLY'S GUN

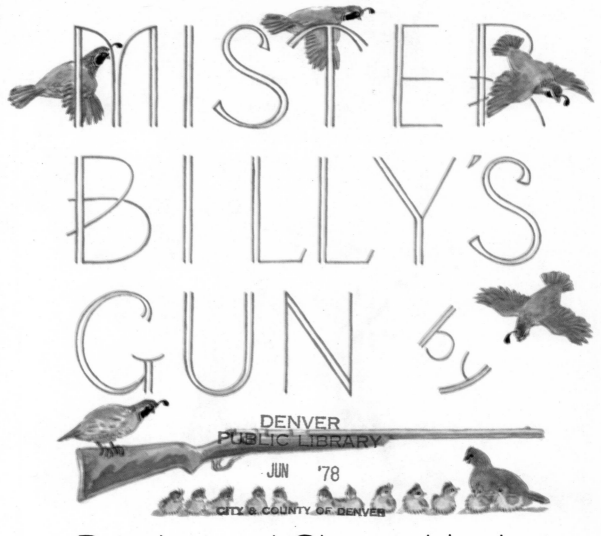

MISTER BILLY'S GUN

by

Berta and Elmer Hader

The Macmillan Company

New York 1960

Affectionately dedicated to
Keith Robinson
and his little cousin
Anne Cameron Horner

Library of Congress catalog card number: 60–12953

First Printing

The Macmillan Company, New York
Brett-Macmillan Ltd., Galt, Ontario

PRINTED IN THE UNITED STATES OF AMERICA

"HEY, GET OUT OF THERE," shouted Mr. Billy as he ran toward his small vegetable garden. A little rabbit eating a tender young lettuce leaf looked up in surprise!

"If I had a GUN, I'd shoot you," sputtered Mr. Billy. The rabbit hopped away. Mr. Billy ran after him, but the rabbit was soon lost from sight in the brambles near the woods.

Mr. Billy walked back to the house. He told Miss Addie, his wife, about the rabbit in the garden. "There won't be any lettuce left soon," he stormed. "What I need is a GUN." Miss Addie looked startled. She didn't like guns.

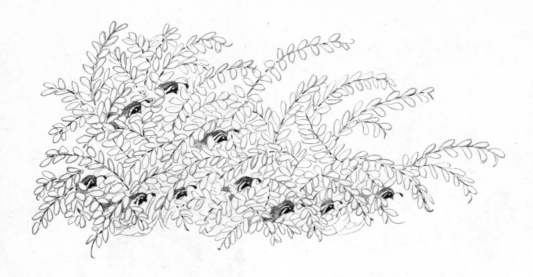

Early the next morning, Mr. Billy went to his garden to plant carrots, beans, peas and some corn. It was a small garden, just big enough for Miss Addie and himself. Mr. Billy didn't know that many bright eyes watched from the nearby woods as he dropped the seeds in the rows. When Mr. Billy had finished planting and had returned to his house, a little band of quail hurried from their hiding place under the laurel, to scratch up and eat the seed in his garden.

But Mr. Billy saw the quail, and he ran from his house shouting angrily, "GET OUT OF THERE! GET OUT OF THERE!" With a flutter of wings, the quail ran into the woods to hide. Mr. Billy returned to the house.

"Now the quail have eaten all the seeds I planted," he said to Miss Addie. "PIGS IN FEATHERS. That's what *they* are. I ought to have a GUN." Mr. Billy was mad.

"Build a fence around the garden," said Miss Addie. "I'll help you." So Mr. Billy and Miss Addie put a wire fence around the garden. Then the quail flew over the fence to eat the seeds and the rabbit dug under the fence to nibble the fresh young lettuce leaves. This made Mr. Billy *very* angry. Luckily, Miss Addie didn't hear what he said.

"Tie bits of rag and small pieces of tin on the fence," said Miss Addie. "They'll blow in the wind, and the tinkle and movement will scare the quail and the rabbit away." Mr. Billy grumbled but he tied rags and pieces of tin on the fence and planted more seed.

For a few days the quail and the rabbit watched the rags and tins flutter in the breeze. Then one quail flew over the fence. He was followed by another quail, then another and another. When the rabbit saw the quail in the garden, he dug a new hole under the fence and came back, too.

The next morning, Mr. Billy looked at his garden. What he saw made him madder than ever. Seeds scratched up, the young lettuce leaves eaten and his garden ruined again. As Mr. Billy walked up the path to his house to get more seed to plant, he muttered over and over, "Get-a-gun, get-a-gun."

Miss Addie heard him. "Put a SCARECROW in the garden," she said quickly. "That will keep the quail and rabbit away. I'll make one out of your old clothes." And she did. The scarecrow looked so much like Mr. Billy that it fooled Mr. Wimple, their nearsighted neighbor.

The scarecrow kept the quail and the rabbit out of the garden and the vegetables grew. Mr. Billy was pleased and he whistled happily as he carefully hoed each row. Then one morning the quail flew over the fence again. The rabbit saw the quail in the garden, so he dug another hole under the fence and enjoyed a nice breakfast of tender bean and carrot tops.

When Mr. Billy saw them, he was furious. He ran out of the house. He was so angry and in such a hurry that he tripped and fell and hurt his leg badly.

Miss Addie heard his cry of pain and ran to help him. She looked at his swollen ankle! "Oh, dear," she said. "Don't move until I get the doctor."

Mr. Billy groaned and grumbled as his neighbors, Mr. Wimple and Dr. Crump, helped Miss Addie put him to bed.

"You have a bad sprain," said the doctor. "It will take time to mend." The doctor gave Miss Addie some pills for Mr. Billy as he left.

"The doctor says you will have to stay in bed until your leg gets better. You won't be able to work in the garden for a long time. I'll buy the vegetables we need at the Davies' farm," said Miss Addie.

"Double darn those quail and that pesky rabbit," said Mr. Billy. He blamed them for his mishap.

Mr. Billy liked to work in his little garden, and he was not happy lying in bed day after day while his leg mended. Though Miss Addie brought books from the village library and neighbors brought him magazines, time passed slowly for Mr. Billy. There were long hours when he just lay in bed and thought. He tried not to think of his garden, for that made him think of the quail and the rabbit, and he blamed them for all his trouble. Miss Addie often heard Mr. Billy thinking out loud.

"I'll get a gun, get-a-gun, get-a-gun," he said over and over. Miss Addie decided she must do something to change his thoughts.

So one morning Miss Addie put her bird-feeder just outside the window near Mr. Billy's bed. "Now you can watch the birds," she said. "They will be company for you."

At first, Mr. Billy just glanced at the song sparrows and the jays that came to the feeder. When he began to save crumbs from his breakfast doughnuts and pieces of bread from his lunch at noon, Miss Addie was pleased. Mr. Billy scattered these extra treats on the lawn below the window, and now he looked forward to the visits of the birds to the feeder.

Watching the birds outside the window helped pass time for Mr. Billy while his leg healed. One morning he saw two quail join the birds eating crumbs on the lawn. Then a rabbit hopped into view. The rabbit found a patch of clover to his liking. A gray squirrel joined the party, too.

Then one morning, twelve fluffy little quail marched with their father and mother across the lawn.

"Addie, Addie, come quick, bring seed. There is a family of baby quail on the lawn. Hurry." Mr. Billy had never seen baby quail before. Miss Addie brought a treat of bread crumbs for the newcomers. The quail family came every morning for breakfast and hurried to the lawn whenever Miss Addie called "Here chickie," or Mr. Billy whistled. When they were old enough to fly, the young quail took short flights to the feeder.

Mr. Billy's leg was much better near the end of the summer. He got up from his bed and, with the help of a cane, walked about the house. On his birthday, Miss Addie baked a coconut cake, and a wonderful surprise came as a gift from Mr. Billy's brother. A red hunting cap and a fine new GUN! Mr. Billy was delighted. "Now, we can have a garden," he said to Miss Addie. "I have a GUN to keep the spoilers away."

"A GUN!" said Miss Addie. "How awfff—I mean, that's just what you wanted, isn't it?" Miss Addie was *not* happy about the gun.

When the cool days of fall came, Mr. Billy was able to walk without the help of a cane. Then one morning he read in the paper that the hunting season was open and he smiled happily. Now he could try his new gun. He didn't say a word to Miss Addie, but early the next morning, he put on his warm coat and the red hunting cap. He loaded his gun and started down the path toward the woods. He chuckled as he recalled boyhood days and happy summer vacations, when he hunted in the woods near his home with his dog Rover. Hunting was fun, though he couldn't remember ever shooting anything with his air rifle except the tin cans he set up as targets on a rock.

When he came to the little vegetable garden, he saw a band of quail hurrying along the path. Mr. Billy raised his gun, but, before he could fire, the quail were all about him. They walked over his feet and circled around and around. The air was filled with their clucking and calling. Mr. Billy stared in wonder. *These quail* were *not* afraid of him. "Gosh," he said to himself. "They must be the quail I've been feeding on the lawn all summer." The quail had followed him along the path. *He* was their FRIEND. He couldn't shoot THEM. Suddenly, Mr. Billy didn't feel like hunting.

Mr. Billy tucked his gun under his arm and started for home. The quail fell in line behind, and they all walked up the path to the little gray house on the brow of the hill. Mr. Billy whistled a merry little tune. "Addie," he called as he drew near the kitchen door. "It's time for doughnuts and coffee."

Mr. Billy hung his new gun over the mantel of the fireplace. Then he hurried to scatter crumbs and seed for the quail on the lawn. The rabbit was in the clover patch eating his breakfast. Miss Addie smiled as she poured the coffee. "Next year," she said, "I will help you plant a garden big enough for us all."